Eva Uses Her Head

by Robert R. O'Brien
illustrated by Linda Kelen

Open Court Publishing Company
Chicago and Peru, Illinois

ISBN 0-8126-1280-9

10 9 8 7 6 5 4 3 2

The Step Problem

Hugo sat on his front step
and moped.
"Such a sad face, Hugo!" said Nana.
"What has made you so sad?"

"I want to invite Eva over,"
said Hugo, "but even if she came,
she wouldn't be able
to get up these steps."

"Do not mope, Hugo," said Nana.
"Use your head. Talk to Eva.
She is used to this kind of problem."

Hugo talked to Eva.
"No problem!" said Eva.
"Let's go!"

"I'm glad you came," said Hugo.
"But these steps are huge.
Will we be able to get inside?"

Eva smiled.
"This is not a hard problem," she said.
"I just use my head!"

10

The Bug Problem

Hugo and Eva sat in Eva's yard.
"Let's go inside," said Hugo.
"These bugs make me itch!"

"I have an idea!" said Eva.

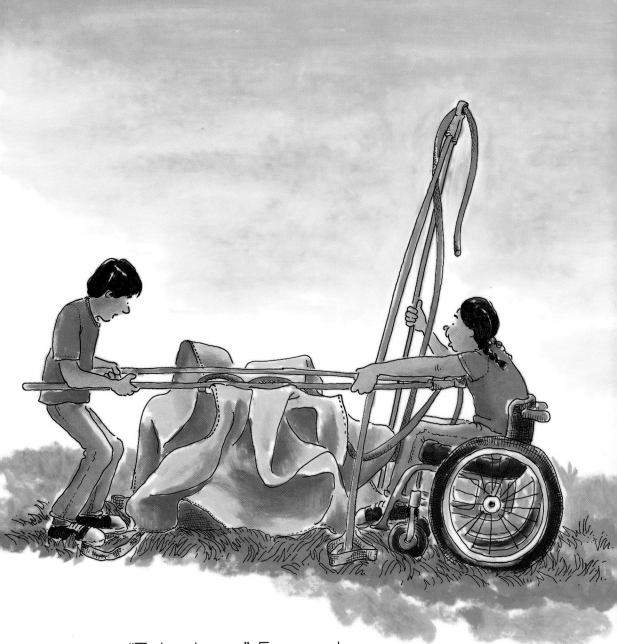

"Take these," Eva said.
She held out two poles.

"What are these for?" asked Hugo.

13

"These poles go here," said Eva,
"and those go next to you."

"Then what is the rope for?" asked Hugo.

14

"I will pull on this end of the rope,"
said Eva, "and you pull on that end."

Eva and Hugo pulled on the rope.

"We made a tent!" said Hugo.

"Yes, we used our heads!"
said Eva, "but let's be quick
and get inside.
These bugs make me itch!"

16